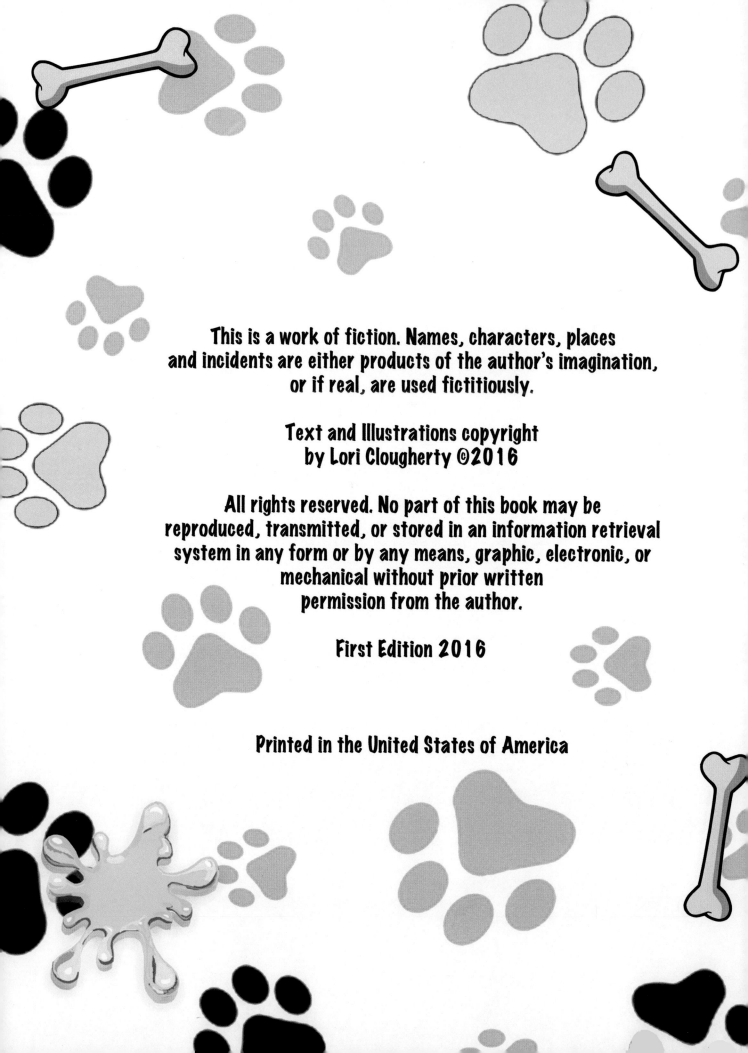

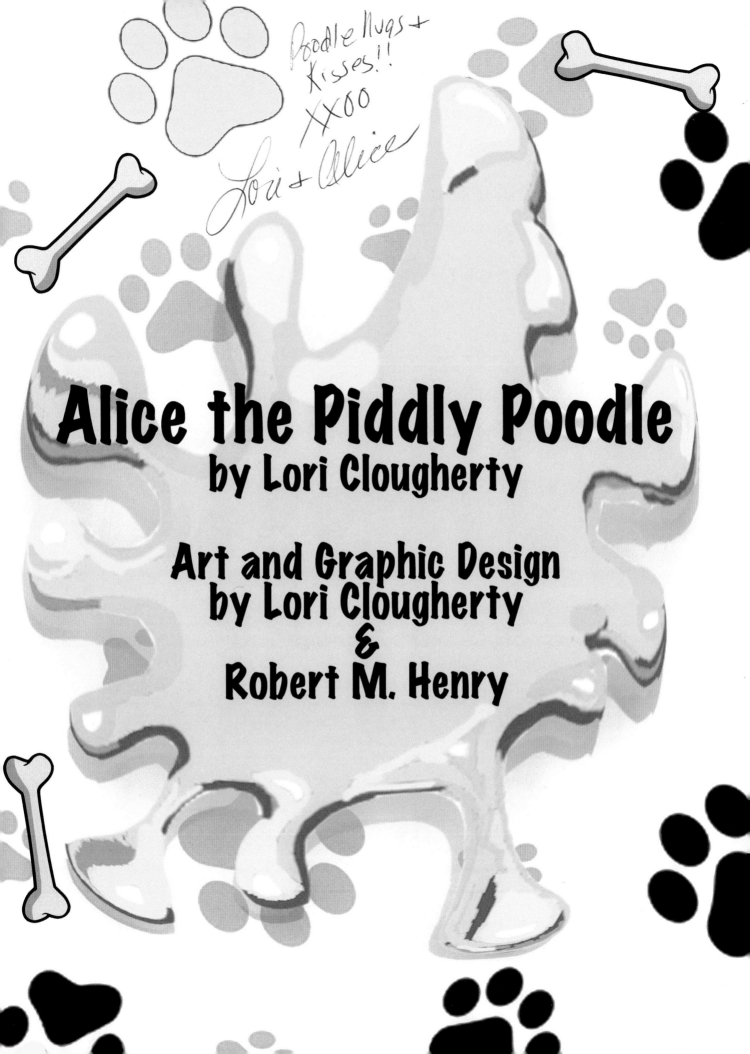

Poodle Hugs +
Kisses!!
XXOO
Lori + Alice

Alice the Piddly Poodle
by Lori Clougherty

Art and Graphic Design
by Lori Clougherty
&
Robert M. Henry

Dedication

For Mark, Elaina,
and Alice (of course)

- L. A. C.

For Coda and Emily. Hugs!

- Alice

Alice is a 10-pound miniature French poodle with a larger than life personality. She gets compliments everywhere she goes. Her favorite compliment is, "I don't even like little dogs but I'll make an exception for Alice."

Alice has a lot of friends!

Jordan

Coda

Sophie

Even a cat!

Tony

3

When Alice was 3 she took a terrible tumble! At the animal hospital Dr. Eva said, "Alice has a ruptured disk in her back and her back legs are paralyzed. She must have surgery right away! There is a chance that Alice will NEVER be able to walk again!"

I fell going up these steps, hurt my back and could not walk!

6

Oh my!
Do you think I
might
need to use
doggie wheels
to get around?!

1

Other things were much improved!

Maybe some music will cheer you up!

Who let the dogs out? Who, who, who, who?!

Sounds great!

Dr. Eva said, "Now Alice needs to go to physical therapy to make her back legs stronger."

Let's start by splashing in the whirlpool!

Look! I'm doing the doggie paddle!

12

Alice took nice long walks on the water treadmill!

Someone STOP this crazy thing!

13

Alice even walked with tiny ankle weights!

All of this physical therapy is "RUFF", but my legs are getting stronger and stronger!

Between physical therapy and check-ups Alice was at the animal hospital so often that everybody working there knew her.

Alice was standing in the canoe!

Alice was even standing on the paddle board!!

17

Alice's humans quickly learned to keep their shoes on!

Maybe acupuncture would help, after all it couldn't hurt.

Can't hurt WHO?! I'm on pins and needles here!

21

When she goes to see Dr. Eva, ALICE PIDDLES!

It would be "BLADDER" if I didn't piddle!

When she meets other dogs, ALICE PIDDLES!

So ha"PEE" to see you Sophie!

23

Alice's humans are hoping for a piddly poodle cleaning product endorsement deal.

27

Perhaps her name should be changed to Puddles!

Puddles the Piddly Poodle! That's me! "Oui!" "Oui!"

29

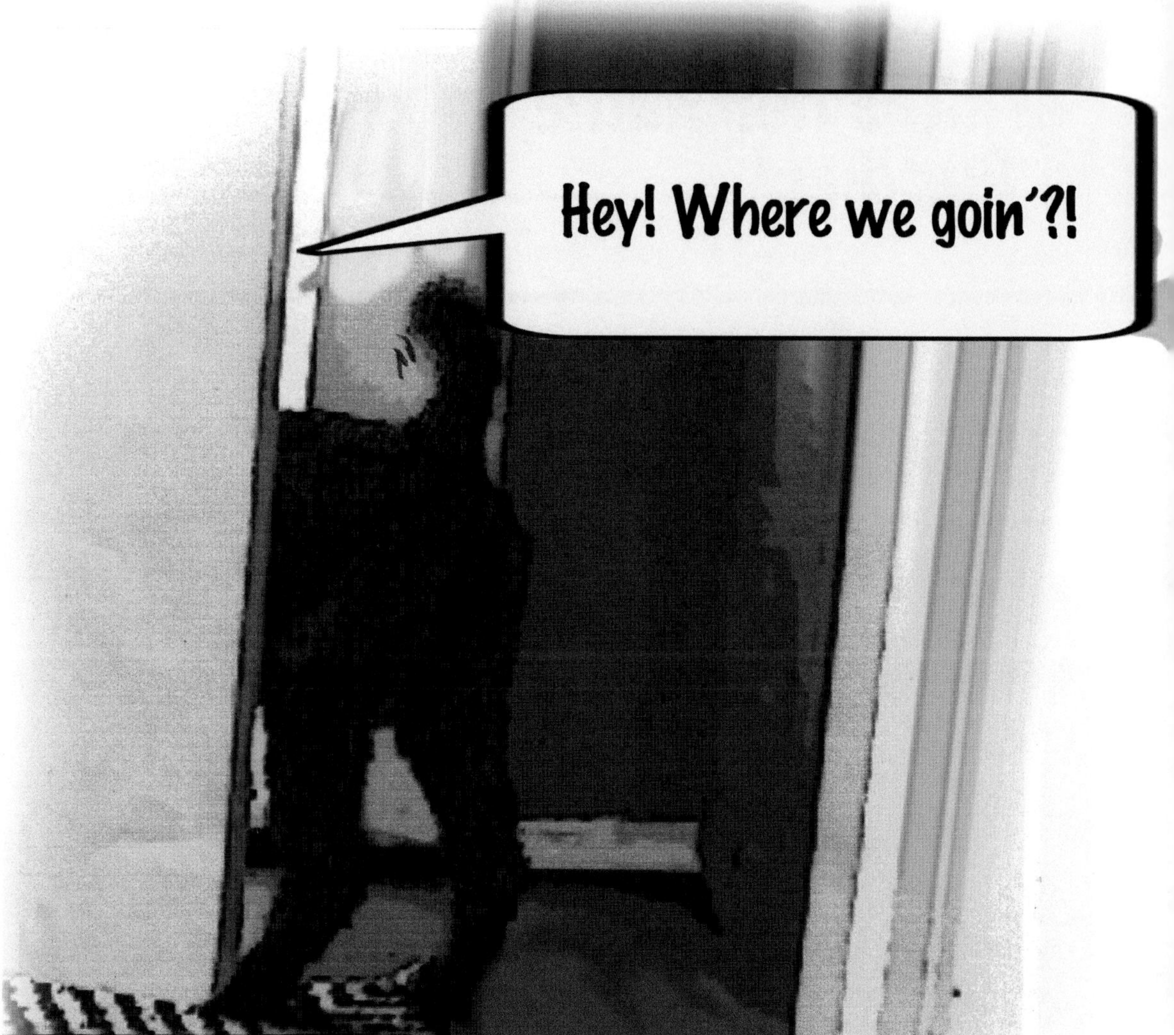

The End

About the Author

Lori Clougherty always knew that the story of Alice's unfortunate accident and remarkable recovery was interesting. She also realized that having a piddly poodle could be horrifying or funny. She chose funny! After all, nothing gets a person through tough times better than potty humor!

About the Inspiration

Alice is now **8** years old. She continues to amaze and entertain as she charms her way through life. And yes, she still piddles!

Made in the USA
Middletown, DE
04 August 2019